IT'S GEORGE!

Story by **Miriam Cohen**
Pictures by **Lillian Hoban**

A Young Yearling Book

Published by
Dell Publishing
a division of
Bantam Doubleday Dell Publishing Group, Inc.
666 Fifth Avenue
New York, New York 10103

ISBN: 0-440-40198-4

Reprinted by arrangement with William Morrow & Company, Inc.,
on behalf of Greenwillow Books.

Printed in the United States of America
July 1989

10 9 8 7 6 5 4 3 2 1
W

FOR ALL THE GEORGES

George was writing something. "What *does* it say?" he asked Jim.

"I don't know. What *does* it say?" Jim said.

Anna Maria looked. "It doesn't say anything, because he can't write. He is D-U-M," Anna Maria announced.

"So what? He's still good!" said Jim.
"You don't know everything!" Paul said.
  But everybody knew that Anna Maria
  was the smartest in First Grade.

Some of the kids tried to help George.
"Just do it like this," Jim said.
"Try, man," said Willy and Sammy.
"You can do it!"

But Danny shook his head. "He'll *never* get it,"
he said.
And Anna Maria said, "You can't *get* smart. You
just are or you aren't."

But George was better than anybody
at taking care of the class hamster.
It never bit him.

And he always fed the fish
just the right amount.

One day everybody was working on projects. Jim and Paul were doing "The Worst Dinosaur! Tyrannosaurus Rex!"

Margaret and Sara were making up
math puzzles.
Louie was drawing a map of a city.
And Anna Maria was writing a book
with chapters.

George was working by himself on a secret project. The secret was that he couldn't think of a project.

"Danny, why don't you work with George?"
the teacher said.
"I want to work with Sammy," Danny said.
And he ran to Sammy's table.

The next day, George did not come to school.
Just before lunch, the principal came in.

"I have a big surprise for First Grade.
To find out what it is, you will have to
watch Channel 3 at four o'clock this afternoon."

After school, Jim and Paul went
to Jim's house, and Jim's mother
made them popcorn to eat.

At four o'clock, the news came on.
The announcer said, "Good afternoon.
This is News 3 at Four.

"A little boy in our city leaves his house early
every morning, so that on his way to school
he can visit with a friend of his who lives alone.

"That friend is 79-year-old Henry Emmons.
Every morning Henry and his young friend
sit on the front porch, rock in their chairs,
and wave at the people driving to work.

"But let's go to that front porch, where our reporter, Angela Simms, is talking to that little boy. He is six-and-a-half-year-old George Jenkins."

"It's George!" Jim and Paul yelled.

The reporter was saying, "Tell us what happened this morning, George."
"Mr. Emmons fell down off the rocker and closed his eyes. I tried to make him get up, but he wouldn't."

"And then what happened, George?"
"I called 911 on the telephone.
 I told them Mr. Emmons was sick,
 and they should come to his house."

"And the Rescue Squad did come, didn't it,
George? It came in time to save Mr. Emmons,
who is feeling much better, thanks to his smart
young friend. Thank you, George. Now, back to
News 3 at Four."

The next morning, at a special assembly for the whole school, the principal made a speech about George.

"This young man knew just the right thing to do. He saved his friend's life."

All the kids and the teacher were smacking George on the back and hugging him.

Then a reporter came to take George's picture for the newspaper. Anna Maria stood next to George. "He's in *my* class," she said.

The reporter put George and the whole
First Grade in front of the school flag.
"Hold it! Smile!"

And the picture in the paper showed George
and all his friends looking happy and proud.